LUST TO DUST

ZAKIR JAWED BHATTI

ISBN: 978-1-0691981-0-5

To my lovely wife, who made me what I am today.

*To my mom, whose love, care, guidance gave me
courage to pursue my dreams.*

Table of Contents

Chapter 1: A Life at the Crossroads 5

Chapter 2: Disillusionment under Bollywood 8

Chapter 3: Love Withers before it Blossoms 11

Chapter 4: A Missed Connection 17

Chapter 5: A Brother's Silent Pining 23

Chapter 6: New Bride Tries to Break the Ice 27

Chapter 7: Shared Memories Fuel a Moment of Madness ... 31

Chapter 8: Dance between Desire and Conscience Rages ... 35

Chapter 9: Deeper in Desire's Tangled Web 39

Chapter 10: A Family's Shattered Peace 43

Chapter 11: House Divided 47

Chapter 12: A New Dawn, A New Beginning in the Desert 50

Chapter 13: A Step Forward 54

Chapter 14: The Weight of Sin 57

Chapter 15: A Seed of Hope 61

Chapter 16: Lust on Skype takes Flight 63

Chapter 17: A Forced Hand 70

Chapter 18: Allure of Forbidden Fruit 73

Chapter 19: A Fractured Heart 76

Chapter 20: A Virtual Deception 79

Chapter 21: Tempest of Passion 83

Chapter 22: A Fractured Commitment 90

Chapter 23: The Price of Betrayal 93

Chapter 24: A Digital Delusion 95

Chapter 25: An Illusion Finally Shattered 99

Chapter 26: The Weight of Regret 102

Chapter 27: It's The Time of Reckoning 107

Chapter 1

A Life at the Crossroads

AUGUST 13, 2023 (PRESENT DAY)

Usman, a broad-shouldered Pakistani man pushing his late twenties, paced the length and breadth of the terrace, a caged lion yearning for escape.

Barely 20 minutes ago, he had slammed the front door shut and sped up the stairs to the top of the ramshackle structure, seeking refuge from the claustrophobic feeling that choked him in his parents' modest 5-room apartment on the building's first floor.

The weight of perceived failures, one tragic love story after another, pressed heavily on him.

His crestfallen face mirrored the despair in his heart, a relentless ache that fueled a singular, destructive purpose. The air grew thick with anticipation as the hour approached midnight.

Below Usman's building, as far as one's eyes could see, the town of Sialkot, a thriving industrial town in Pakistan's Punjab province, pulsed with celebratory fervor.

Its residents, like their brethren all over the country, were readying to ring in the 76th anniversary of their nation's Independence Day.

Buildings, draped in the emerald green and white of the national flag, twinkled with festive lights, casting a warm glow on the bustling streets.

Yet, on his rooftop perch, Usman felt utterly isolated, the joyous preparations a stark contrast to the desolate landscape of his own heart.

He threw his hands up in the air, his voice battling the wind, "It's all over! What the hell have I done with my life? Not even thirty, and this feels like the end!"

His words were lost in the roar of the approaching storm, a lonely cries swallowed by the vast emptiness.

Driven by a restless despair, he rushed to the railing, his gaze plunging down into the street five floors below.

Was this it, then? Was this all life had to offer, a tapestry woven with unfulfilled dreams and gnawing regret at failing to find true love?

The thought was a bitter pill to swallow, leaving a taste of ashes in his mouth.

The time had come for Usman to end his misery by jumping from the rooftop. The usually vibrant town, a kaleidoscope of life and light, seemed muted tonight, the streetlamps casting long, skeletal shadows. The scent of rain, metallic and fresh, filled his lungs, a stark contrast to the turmoil churning within him.

The thought of ending his suffering, of leaping from the rooftop, becomes increasingly tempting.

Suddenly, Usman remembers about the letter his sister, Farida, had entrusted him. He pulls the letter from his pocket, his fingers trembling as he opens the envelope…

The storm raged on, relentless and unforgiving, yet Usman stood tall, his silhouette stark against the weeping sky.

The rain washed away the grime of despair, leaving behind a raw determination.

No, this wasn't the end. It was a turning point, a chance to rewrite the narrative.

The storm might rage, but he wouldn't be swept away. He would weather it, emerge stronger, and carve his own path, even if the journey ahead was shrouded in uncertainty.

With newfound resolve, Usman turned away from the railing, the rain drumming a rhythm of hope on his back. He had a story to write, and it wouldn't be one of defeat.

It would be a story of resilience, of rising from the ashes, of reclaiming his life one storm-drenched step at a time. The journey had just begun.

Chapter 2

Disillusionment under Bollywood

A WEEK BEFORE THE PRESENT DAY

Usman, a solitary figure in his modest abode, has just finished a mundane chore: stocking the kitchen. Now, as he reclines on his bed, his mind wanders back to a simpler time, a time of youthful innocence and cinematic dreams.

It's a sweltering summer day in Karachi, 2008. A solitary fan whirls lazily above young Usman, offering little respite from the relentless heat.

Lost in the flickering glow of the television screen, he gazes upon the iconic figure of Shah Rukh Khan, his face etched with the universal language of heartbreak.

The Bollywood epic, *Veer-Zaara*, with its sweeping romance and star-crossed lovers, has ensnared the boy's heart.

The final credits roll, and Usman is jolted back to the present. A sigh escapes his lips as he contemplates the stark contrast between the idealistic boy he once was and the cynical man he has become.

The innocent dreamer, once captivated by the magic of cinema and the promise of love, has been replaced by a jaded soul, disillusioned by life's harsh realities.

"A naive fool," he mutters to himself, his voice heavy with self-derision. "Believing in fairy tales, in love at first sight."

He recalls the countless hours spent devouring Bollywood romances – *Kal Ho Naa Ho, Dilwale Dulhania Le Jayenge, Kuch Kuch Hota Hain* and *Veer-Zaara*.

Each film, with its idealized portrayals of love, had painted a rosy picture of the world, a world far removed from his own.

"Fucking romance," he scoffs, his voice laced with bitterness.

"A cruel illusion, a deceptive mirage." His heart, once tender and hopeful, has been scarred by a series of failed relationships, each one chipping away at his belief in love.

A wry smile plays on his lips as he reflects on his youthful naiveté. "I truly believed in Shah Rukh Khan's promises," he admits.

"I thought love was as simple as a grand gesture or a heartfelt declaration." But the harsh realities of life have shattered his illusions.

Usman slams his fist on the floor, the sound sharp in the quiet room.

"Believe me," he spits, his young voice laced with bitterness, "Bloody romance only exists in movies."

Just as Usman switches the lights on in the room, a memory flickers to life – a warmth spreading through him despite the cynicism that's taken root. It's the memory of his "first love," a girl from his tuition class eighteen years ago.

How could he forget the spark, the stolen glances, the whispered dreams? How could he deny the reality of love after experiencing it firsthand?

But then, a shadow falls across the memory. The "treacherous Universe," as he bitterly terms it, intervened, bringing their innocent romance to a sudden end.

The disillusionment washes back over him, leaving a bitter taste in his mouth.

Chapter 3

Love Withers before it Blossoms

In 2009 the relentless Karachi sun beat down on fourteen-year-old Usman as he and Urooj, a girl with eyes the color of a summer sky, emerged from their houses across the dusty street.

Their backpacks, bulging with textbooks, seemed impossibly heavy on their slender shoulders. Though heading to different schools, their paths converged at the corner, where they'd share a silent greeting – a shy smile from Usman, a nonchalant flick of her long brown braid from Urooj.

Usman had admired Urooj since they were children, her beauty surpassing anything he'd seen on television. Her figure, already beginning to mature at their age, was a constant source of fascination for him.

He'd spend hours sketching portraits in his notebook, capturing the way her full lips curved upwards in a smile and the way her laughter danced in her bright blue eyes.

Afternoons found both Usman and Urooj hunched over desks at the same private tuition center.

One sweltering day, as Usman sat slumped beside his goofy friend Arman, the latter nudged him with his elbow, his gaze fixed on Urooj.

"Isn't she something?" Arman sighed dreamily, his voice thick with teenage infatuation. "Like a movie star in the making."

Usman, his cheeks flushing a warm pink, acknowledged, "Yeah, she's Urooj. Lives right next door actually."

Arman's eyes widened. "Seriously? You never mentioned that!" He slumped forward, confessing, "The truth is, Usman, I think I'm smitten. I can't seem to get her off my mind."

Usman, battling a surge of possessiveness that surprised him, replied in a voice devoid of emotion, "You can have her. She's all yours."

Confused, Arman bristled. "What do you mean 'mine'? She's not some possession you can just hand over!"

Usman's voice sharpened defensively. "If she were, you wouldn't stand a chance. But the truth is," he admitted sheepishly, "I'm too much of a coward. Can't even bring myself to say hello."

Fueled by Usman's confession and a newfound sense of courage, Arman approached Urooj after their class.

He attempted a grand gesture, mimicking a scene from a popular Bollywood movie, hoping to impress her. The sight was so awkward it made Usman cringe.

"Hi Urooj," Arman greeted her, his voice cracking slightly as he tried to pull off a suave, wide-armed gesture.

Urooj, completely oblivious to his intentions, raised an eyebrow in confusion. The unwanted attention, especially from someone she hadn't even noticed during the past six months of classes, seemed to mildly irritate her.

Sensing her coldness, Arman stammered, his confidence melting faster than an ice cube in the Karachi heat. His feet felt glued to the pavement, rendering him speechless. Urooj, with a dismissive shrug and a hint of annoyance, simply walked away, leaving a crestfallen Arman in his wake.

Usman, unable to stifle a smirk, approached his dejected friend. "See? Not so easy, is it?" he said, a touch of mockery in his voice. "I didn't even manage a decent conversation." Feeling a surge of sympathy, he added, "Come on, let's get some pakoras. Mom just made a fresh batch. Maybe on a full stomach, you can come up with a better plan to win Urooj's affection."

The next day, however, fate intervened in a way that left Usman speechless. As they exited the tuition center, Urooj surprised him by calling out, "Hey you!"

Usman froze, heart pounding in his chest. "M-me?" he stammered, unsure if he'd heard correctly.

"Hell, no, I'm squint-eyed. Who else?" she teased, her voice softer than usual. "I need a favor. Can I borrow your English grammar notes?"

Usman felt his heart skip a beat. Here was his dream girl, the one who occupied his waking thoughts and even infiltrated his dreams, talking directly to him! "S-sure, of course!" he stammered, fumbling with the straps of his backpack In his haste to retrieve the notebook.

His nervousness, a constant companion whenever he was around Urooj, caused the contents to spill out in a chaotic mess of pens, pencils, and loose papers scattered on the sidewalk like fallen dominoes.

"Oh dear, I'm so sorry!" he exclaimed, mortified by his clumsiness and feeling like a complete klutz. "Let me just…" He squatted down awkwardly, his face burning with embarrassment, to gather his scattered belongings.

Urooj, however, seemed amused by his flustered reaction. "For a moment there, I thought you were trying to impress me with a magic trick," she teased, her tone light and playful, a stark contrast to Usman's internal turmoil. "But seriously though, just the notes for now, please."

Usman, finally managing to corral his belongings back into his bag, sheepishly handed her the notebook. "I'll return them tomorrow," she promised, a hint of a smile lingering on her lips. The way she said it, with a casualness that sent a thrill shooting through him, made it sound more like a promise to meet again rather than a simple exchange of school supplies.

The next day, Usman waited impatiently by his doorstep for what felt like an eternity.

Every rustle of leaves, every creak of a floorboard from inside the house had him jumping up, his heart pounding in his chest. Finally, just as he was about to give up hope, he spotted Urooj approaching from down the street.

As Usman opened the door, Urooj politely declined his offer to come inside, explaining that her parents were waiting to take her out for dinner.

A pang of rejection, sharp and unexpected, pierced his heart. He mumbled a dismissive, "No problem," trying to mask his disappointment.

Urooj, oblivious to the storm of emotions brewing inside him, instructed him to review some points she'd highlighted in the notes before turning to leave. "There are some things I need help with," she added, her voice barely a whisper. "Maybe we can go over them sometime?"

Usman's spirits soared. Here was his chance, a potential invitation to spend time with her alone. But before he could muster the courage to ask when, Urooj was already walking away, leaving him breathless with a mixture of excitement and nervousness.

Examining the notes later, Usman discovered a love letter slipped in by Urooj, confessing her feelings for him. The words swam before his eyes, a beautiful, unexpected dream come true. It took a moment for the message to fully register.

He rushed to his room, a whirlwind of emotions swirling in his head – visions of red roses, stolen kisses, and tender moments under the Karachi sky – only to be interrupted by his parents discussing the arrival of movers who would be packing for their upcoming relocation.

Early the next morning, a truck stood parked outside Usman's house, its empty belly waiting to be filled with the contents of their life. His parents carried boxes, their faces etched with a mixture of sadness and excitement for their new beginning.

As his family prepared to move to the distant town of Sialkot, a helpless Usman watched his first love wither on the vine, before it ever had a chance to bloom.

The cruel twist of fate stole his chance at happiness, leaving behind a bittersweet ache in his heart, a memory that would forever be tinged with the dusty hues of a summer in Karachi.

Chapter 4

A Missed Connection

Clad impeccably for a wedding, the 20-year-old Usman appraised his reflection with a critical eye. He meticulously smoothed his hair, then dabbed cologne on himself – a subtle indulgence amidst the pre-wedding frenzy. The tranquillity shattered as Salman, his boisterous cousin a few years his senior, barged into the room with rambunctious energy.

"What in tarnation are you doing? Why the interminable delay? You're not the damn groom, so get a move on!" Salman exclaimed.

"Just give me a moment to finish grooming," Usman retorted with a hint of sharpness.

"Hahaha! Dude, you must harbor a hidden feminine side," Salman chuckled. "Only women dedicate such an inordinate amount of time to beautification."

Moments later, they squeezed onto a bus overflowing with fellow wedding guests, bound for Nawan Pind, the remote location for the festivities.

Halfway through the journey, the bus lurched onto a narrow, unpaved road, transforming the ride into a bone-jarring experience.

As the bus sputtered to a halt, Usman's voice rose above the cacophony of disgruntled passengers. "Where the devil are we?" he shrieked.

"Looks like we've reached Nawan Pind," Salman said, peering through the partially shut window.

Usman squinted out as well. "Dude, I see only a smattering of houses here," he remarked.

"So our cousin Shahid is marrying a girl from this God-forsaken backwater? You've got to be kidding me," Salman scoffed.

"Must be a tribal princess he's snagged. But our rotten luck! There's no way we'll find any eligible ladies in this desolate place."

Their dismay deepened upon arrival at the wedding venue. Two large tents stood apart, one designated exclusively for women, the other for men.

Salman, whose disappointment had morphed into full-blown frustration, grumbled, "If I had known about this segregated seating arrangement, I wouldn't have boarded this infernal wedding bus in the first place."

Usman mirrored his sentiment with a sigh. "To think I wasted two precious hours on my hair only to be greeted by this two- tent fiasco."

For a seemingly interminable period, the cousins loitered outside the men's tent, cursing their fate and the antiquated wedding customs. As they droned on with their complaints, a vision emerged from the women's tent, accompanied by a group of her friends.

Her beauty rivaled Snow White's. Her hips swayed with a subtle sensuality, her long, coffee-colored tresses cascaded down her back, brushing against her buttocks. A tight-fitting, embroidered pink kameez

accentuated her voluptuous figure. Her emerald eyes, framed by thick lashes and perfectly groomed brows, were the crowning glory of her breathtaking visage.

As the group of women passed the young men, the captivating beauty locked eyes with Usman and offered him a knowing smile.

"Dude, look! She just smiled at you!" Salman nudged Usman excitedly.

"What smile?" Usman feigned nonchalance.

"Not just any smile, you dolt," Salman countered. "That was a smile that practically screamed, 'I want you!' How I wish it had been me!"

Usman scoffed, shaking his head. "Are you crazy? Even if you're right, she must be blind. How could someone as exquisite as her be interested in someone like me?"

"Let's follow her," Salman suggested, a mischievous glint in his eyes.

They discreetly trailed the woman, who seemed increasingly aware of their pursuit. She kept glancing back over her shoulder. Finally, Usman turned to Salman, a mixture of confusion and apprehension clouding his features. "Now what?" he asked.

"Go talk to her! Ask for her number," Salman urged, nudging Usman again, who stumbled and landed flat on his face.

"I didn't tell you to grovel at her feet, cousin," Salman said with a chuckle, extending a hand to help Usman up. "Just approach her and say something witty. Break the ice with a clever remark."

Usman, however, remained rooted to the spot, paralyzed by shyness. "I can't just blurt out a request for her number," he stammered, a note of defeat creeping into his voice.

"Then give her yours!" Salman countered. "She'll definitely contact you."

"How?" Usman asked, bewildered.

"You simpleton! Write it down on a piece of paper and hand it to her. It's that easy," Salman explained, exasperation lacing his tone.

"I've never done anything like that before," Usman confessed, his eyes filled with dejection.

A vein pulsed visibly on Salman's temple as he addressed his cousin. "Usman, seize the opportunity, my friend! Observe the young lady across the way. The furtive glances she throws in your direction speak volumes. Don't be a timorous fool, Usman. This woman is an ethereal vision! Act with haste before she vanishes from your grasp entirely!"

Undeterred by Salman's impassioned diatribe, Usman embarked on a seemingly futile quest to procure a pen.

"Are you absolutely serious, Salman?" he sputtered in exasperation. "What kind of archaic era have we stumbled into? Have pens become extinct artifacts?"

A hearty guffaw erupted from Salman. "Easy there, scholar! We are at a joyous wedding celebration, not a university lecture hall. Unless, of course, you harbor a secret desire to spend the rest of your days receiving instruction from that captivating creature."

With a resigned sigh, Usman entered a nearby convenience store and emerged triumphantly with a pen. He meticulously inscribed his number on a scrap of paper, his heart pounding a frantic rhythm against his ribs. They retraced their steps towards the opulent tent housing the female guests.

Usman's gaze became fixated on his object of desire, a radiant vision amidst a gaggle of friends, their laughter tinkling like wind chimes. Suddenly, he realized Salman had vanished without a trace.

A tense ten minutes crawled by before Salman reappeared, a mischievous glint in his eyes. "Information has been gleaned, my friend, concerning your newfound amour. Her name, it turns out, is Kajal. But brace yourself, Usman, for this may come as a shock – she is related to you! A daughter of your mother's cousin, to be precise."

Usman could feel the color drain from his face. "Salman," he croaked, his voice thick with despair, "your revelation has dealt a devastating blow to my heart. This complicates matters considerably. If Kajal has no romantic interest in me, and worse, is offended by my audacity, her family will undoubtedly seek retribution from my mother. I am utterly doomed!"

Years later, the memory of this missed opportunity would continue to torment Usman. The image of Kajal, forever out of reach, would be a constant source of regret, a phantom love that haunted him into the foreseeable future.

Chapter 5

A Brother's Silent Pining

21-year-old Usman, now sporting a neatly trimmed beard that gave him a more mature look, sat hunched over his studies in his room. The sounds of animated chatter filtered in from next door, where the rest of the family - his older brothers and their wives, his sisters and their husbands - were gathered in the main TV-viewing hall. The topic of discussion, as Usman soon learned, was the upcoming marriage of his younger brother, Farhan.

Usman's mother, Shahida, took center stage. "I think we should get Usman's opinion on Farhan marrying before him," she suggested.

Anwar, Usman's father, relayed the message to Usman, who reluctantly joined the family gathering. "We're discussing Farhan's marriage," his father began.

"Usman, you're still in college, whereas Farhan's already settled with a job. Since you two are the only ones left single, it might be best for Farhan, financially speaking, to get married first."

"Why ask me?" Usman replied with a hint of disapproval in his voice. "Marriage wasn't really on my mind anyway."

Anwar, a touch impatient with his son's nonchalance, retorted, "Listen, smart aleck, I was just explaining the situation." He then turned to his daughters, seeking their approval.

The sisters, after exchanging a knowing look, nodded in agreement. "You're right, Dad," they chorused.

With the family consensus settled, Anwar declared, "It's decided then. Farhan will marry first."

Usman, clearly miffed, mumbled, "I'm going back to my studies. Please don't disturb me again… with these silly marriage talks."

Weeks later, the family meeting that had set Farhan's marriage in motion bore fruit. A proposal arrived for Farhan, and as fate would cruelly twist the knife, the girl he was to marry was Kajal, the very same girl Usman had secretly cherished since their chance encounter a year ago at a wedding reception.

News of the proposal reached Usman during a teatime family gathering. Shahida, her eyes twinkling with excitement, passed him a photograph of the girl Farhan was to marry. "Her name is Kajal," she announced.

Usman's world tilted on its axis. The moment his eyes met Kajal's smiling face in the photograph, his breath hitched, and his heart plummeted.

His hands grew numb, and he watched helplessly as the picture slipped from his grasp, fluttering to the floor. Despite the overwhelming urge to cry out in despair, Usman managed to compose himself.

"I… I see," he stammered, forcing his gaze away from the fallen photo as he retrieved it and handed it back to his mother.

Shahida, oblivious to the storm raging within her son, patted his shoulder sympathetically. "Don't worry about it, son.

You're at a crucial stage in your life, focusing on college. Farhan's settled with his job, and your turn to marry, Inshallah, will come soon enough."

Usman, unable to bear the charade any longer, rose abruptly and strode out of the house. He found solace on the rooftop, where he surrendered to a torrent of tears. "Why, Allah? Why me?" he cried out, his voice hoarse with anguish, his eyes pleading with the leaden sky above to share his grief.

Exactly a week later, on a sunny Sunday afternoon, a knock on the door echoed through Usman's house. Usman's ears perked up at the murmur of familiar voices. It was Kajal's family, and they had come to discuss the wedding preparations with his own.

Usman's heart lurched. He couldn't bear the thought of facing Kajal, not when his heart ached so intensely at the prospect of losing her forever. An invisible force seemed to root him to the spot. A dreadful premonition washed over Usman as he braced himself.

With a deep breath, he crept towards the living room door, his heart hammering a frantic rhythm against his ribs.

He peeked through the sliver of an opening, and his breath caught in his throat.

Kajal stood at the doorway, a radiant vision in a simple salwar kameez, her smile as warm and inviting as the summer sun. The sight of her sent a dagger deep into his heart, a fresh wave of despair threatening to drown him.

The day of Farhan's wedding arrived, a vibrant celebration steeped in the rich traditions of a Sialkot Punjabi wedding.

The air thrummed with joyous music, the scent of exotic spices filled the air, and guests adorned in colorful finery danced with abandon.

Amidst the revelry, Usman, a ghost at his own brother's wedding, moved through the ceremony with a vacant expression. He had volunteered to help with the catering, a task that kept him away from the festivities and allowed him to steal moments of solitude.

When it came time for the family photoshoot, Shahida discreetly nudged her husband, asking him to fetch Usman. As Usman stood awkwardly beside the beaming newlyweds, Farhan and Kajal, the rest of the family gathered around them, a potent cocktail of emotions churned within him.

He fought back tears that threatened to spill over, the joy of his brother's union a stark contrast to the hollowness in his own heart.

The moment the photographer signaled the end of the photo session, Usman found himself retreating behind a nearby stage curtain. There, hidden from view, he allowed the dam to break, tears of unspoken love and sacrifice cascading down his face.

Chapter 6

New Bride Tries to Break the Ice

Bound by tradition in their Pakistani household, Kajal, the new bride, navigated the unfamiliar territory of serving meals to her husband's elder sibling, Usman.

Stepping into his room with a plateful of chicken curry and rice, she found him gazing impassively at the ceiling.

"Take it back," Usman mumbled, his voice devoid of emotion. "I'm not hungry."

Kajal's heart sank. Retreating to the kitchen, she placed the untouched food in the refrigerator, a knot of disappointment tightening in her stomach.

A few minutes later, the sound of the refrigerator door opening again startled her. It was Usman, helping himself to the very meal he'd just refused.

Bemusement colored Kajal's voice as she addressed him. "Just a few minutes ago, you wouldn't have this. What changed?"

Usman's response was a curt, "So what?" The conversation, on the verge of blossoming, wilted, leaving Kajal with a helpless shrug. She retreated to her room, her frustrations spilling out to Farhan, her husband, who was engrossed in a television program.

"What's wrong with your brother?" Kajal exclaimed, throwing her arms up in exasperation. "He wouldn't even talk to me!"

Farhan dismissed her concerns with a casual wave of his hand. "He's always like this. Leave him alone. Maybe some seasonal thing, like a woman's period," he added with a misfired attempt at humor.

Weeks later, Shahida entered the room where Usman was glued to his favorite TV serial. "Farhan called," she announced. "He'll be late from work. Usman, you'll have to pick Kajal up from your aunt Khalida's place. It's getting late."

Usman's brows furrowed. The prospect of missing the climax of his show was unappealing. "What the hell, Mom? Why do I have to go? You can pick her up," he grumbled.

Shahida's stern gaze silenced any further protest. "Just shut up and go," she commanded. Usman, well aware of the consequences of defying his mother, meekly switched off the TV and left the house.

The walk back home provided an unexpected opportunity for connection. Mustering her courage, Kajal broke the ice. "It's been almost a year since I married your brother," she said, her voice tentative. "Why haven't you spoken to me even once?"

Usman remained silent, his gaze fixed on the dusty path ahead. But Kajal, emboldened by a newfound resolve, pressed on. "I've noticed you're quiet," she continued, a hint of hurt lacing her tone. "But it still hurts that you always ask your other sisters-in-law for things, but never me."

Another uncomfortable silence followed, stretching into what felt like an eternity.

Finally, Usman, surprised by her persistence, mumbled a response. "It's not a big deal to me," he muttered, more to the ground than to her.

Back home, the family gathered in the living room to discuss a wedding invitation.

Shahida, as the matriarch, initiated the conversation, her eyes settling on Usman. "Your uncle Rashid's son, Jamil, is getting married this Saturday," she announced. "We've been invited. I've already spoken to your father, and I hope everyone can join us."

Farhan was the first to respond, his voice laced with apology. "Sorry, Mom, I'm out. I have some urgent work for my boss that needs to be completed by Sunday. I won't be able to make it."

His gaze then shifted to Kajal. "Kajal," he offered, "you can go with the rest of the family."

Kajal, however, hesitated. "I'm not in the mood to go without you," she replied softly. "It wouldn't look right if I went alone. I'll stay behind. There will be other weddings."

Shahida turned to Usman, her brow creased in concern. "And you, Usman?" she inquired.

"Leave me out too," Usman grumbled, his voice thick with irritation.

Shahida's maternal instincts kicked in. "Usman, why don't you want to come?" she prodded.

"I hate weddings," he retorted, his voice laced with defiance.

"Since when?" Shahida pressed.

Usman's reply was flippant. "From this very moment."

Chapter 7

Shared Memories Fuel a Moment of Madness

The morning bustled with pre-wedding activity. Farhan, with a hurried goodbye kiss to Kajal, left for work. The rest of the house, however, was a whirlwind of vibrant sarees, clinking jewelry, and nervous laughter.

Shahida darted out of her room with a frantic cry, "Everyone, a little pep in your step! We don't want to be in standing room only on the bus. And Kajal, darling, we'll be feasting at the wedding, so just whip something up for Farhan, Usman, and yourself."

A flurry of changing into dazzling wedding finery ensued, punctuated by meticulous mirror checks and a liberal application of perfume. Soon, the house emptied, leaving behind a blissful silence and Usman sprawled comfortably on the sofa, seeking solace in a television program.

An hour later, Kajal emerged from the kitchen, bearing a steaming plate of lunch. Usman, momentarily distracted from the flickering screen, began to devour his meal with gusto.

"How is it?" Kajal inquired, her voice gentle.

Usman, with his mouth full, offered a nonchalant, "If I'm eating, it's good."

"Why didn't you join them at the reception?" Kajal asked curiously.

Usman shrugged. "Didn't feel like it, I guess."

Kajal, finding herself drawn to the quiet man, watched him eat, secretly hoping for his approval of her cooking. A sudden smile flitted across Usman's face, catching her eye.

"What has you smiling?" she queried, intrigued.

A reminiscent tone crept into Usman's voice. "Just re-membering the first time I saw you at the wedding in Na-wanpind. Maybe you don't remember, but it was…well, the most embarrassing moment of my life."

A spark of recognition ignited in Kajal's eyes. "Oh, I re-member you alright! And that cousin of ours…Salman, wasn't it? You two followed me around like lost puppies. But why didn't you say hello if you were so smitten?" she teased, a playful glint in her eyes.

Usman chuckled sheepishly. "Shy, I suppose. Afraid to talk to girls. More like, convinced I wasn't good enough to attract anyone."

"Nonsense!" Kajal exclaimed, her voice laced with disbe-lief. "You're quite handsome, actually. Just needed to over-come those pesky shyness demons."

She leaned closer, her tone conspiratorial, "Girls appreci-ate a bold approach, you know. A little conversation goes a long way."

Lost in their conversation, they reveled in the shared memory, a memory that, in reality, never existed. Suddenly, a strange sensation swept over Usman.

A feeling as if someone was whispering secrets into his ear. He whipped his head to the left, only to see his reflection staring back, albeit a slightly grotesque version with a mischievous glint in its eyes.

"Dude," the reflection drawled, "she's totally into you."

Usman scoffed. "What are you talking about? She's my sister-in-law! Married to my brother, and very much in love with him."

His reflection persisted, Its voice dripping with exaggerated incredulity. "Wrong! See how she talks to you? Called you handsome, even! Why would she do that if she wasn't interested?"

The voice continued, Its reasoning twisted and warped. "Besides, who cares about those technicalities? You were clearly her first love, not your brother. Just lean in and kiss her. You know you want to."

Just then, another voice chimed in, this one emanating from his right side. Usman turned to see a celestial version of himself, radiating an air of serenity.

"Don't listen to him, Usman," the angelic figure implored. "He's leading you astray. Kajal is your brother's wife, and you must respect that bond."

Kajal, bewildered by Usman's sudden zoned-out state, nudged him gently. "Usman? Are you alright? You've been staring off into space for a while now."

Concerned, she reached out to touch his forehead, checking for a fever.

In a moment of inexplicable madness, Usman's distorted reflection seemed to win the internal battle. He lunged forward and grabbed Kajal's shoulders, his lips meeting hers in a sudden, unwelcome kiss.

Shocked and hurt, Kajal shoved him away. Usman, overwhelmed by shame and regret, sprinted out of the house, leaving Kajal reeling in his wake.

He wandered mindlessly through the streets, feeling utterly lost. Curses streamed through his mind, directed both at himself and the strange voices that had played him like a cheap fiddle.

As he passed by, the neighbors watched with a mixture of concern and amusement, convinced they'd witnessed a man on the verge of a breakdown.

Little did they know, the true source of his turmoil resided not in the world around him, but in the unsettling battle raging within.

Chapter 8

Dance between Desire and Conscience Rages

Kajal, her kohl-rimmed eyes reddened from a torrent of tears, slumped on the prayer rug. Guilt, a relentless serpent, coiled in her gut. How quickly had innocent flirtation with Usman morphed into this agonizing remorse? Hadn't she been the one to fan the flames of his desire, praising his handsomeness and lingering a touch too long on his forehead, even though it was to check for a fever?

Now, wracked with regret, she pleaded for divine intervention, her whispered prayers echoing in the silent night.

Across the house, sleep eluded Usman. The rhythmic chirping of crickets outside his window served as a mocking counterpoint to the turmoil within.

Restless, he flipped on the television, the flickering images of a live cricket match failing to hold his attention. His mind, a traitor to his conscience, kept straying to the kitchen, where Kajal, undoubtedly lost in a world of her own, kneaded dough for the morning chapattis.

An invisible force, a potent blend of opportunity and suppressed yearning, propelled him towards the kitchen. The devil on his shoulder, a voice smooth as buttered naan, hissed in his ear,

"She's alone. Vulnerable. This is your chance." A flicker of conscience flickered within him, but the devil was a persistent salesman, painting a vivid picture of Kajal's "desirable" state, the loose strands of hair escaping her braid, the curve of her hip accentuated by the rhythmic kneading of the dough. Shame battled with a raw, primal desire that left him hot and cold.

"This is wrong," Usman mumbled, his voice thick with inner conflict.

The devil, sensing his wavering resolve, pressed its advantage. "Everyone's asleep. Take what you've always wanted."

Kajal's heart hammered a frantic tattoo against her ribs as she sensed Usman's presence nearby. A strange mixture of apprehension and a long-dormant yearning coursed through her veins. Before she could voice a protest, Usman's hand shot out, his touch igniting a spark that threatened to consume them both.

His grip tightened, possessive and urgent. His hands, calloused from years of hard jwork, roamed her back, sending shivers down her spine. "I can't control myself," he rasped, his voice husky with desire.

Kajal, caught between surrender and the remnants of her morals, stammered a feeble, "We can't do this." But the words rang hollow, even to her own ears.

"Don't you feel the same?" Usman pleaded, his voice laced with a desperation that mirrored her own.

Their defenses, as fragile as cobwebs in a monsoon wind, crumbled. Tentative kisses escalated quickly, fueled by a forbidden desire that burned hotter with every touch. Just as Usman, his inhibitions dissolving like sugar in hot chai, reached for Kajal's firm breasts, a voice, sharp as a shard of broken glass, shattered the moment.

Kajal lurched back, scrambling to smooth down her clothes as Shahida, Usman's mother, entered the kitchen. Relief, a tidal wave after a harrowing storm, washed over Kajal. Usman, feigning nonchalance, grabbed a water bottle, his throat suddenly parched. Shahida's raised eyebrows and unspoken inquiries hung heavy in the air.

Returning to the prayer room, the weight of their transgression settled on Kajal's shoulders like a shroud. Tears welled up in her eyes, blurring the already indistinct images on the television screen. With trembling hands, she completed her prayer, the words tasting like ashes in her mouth.

Shahida, her perceptive eyes noticing Kajal's distress, reached out a comforting hand. "Is everything alright, beta? Is it something to do with Farhan?"

Kajal lied easily, the words slick on her tongue: "Everything's fine, Mother. I was just seeking forgiveness for my sins."

Shahida squeezed her hand. "Everyone sins, dear. But Allah is forgiving."

As for Usman and Kajal, the weight of their actions hung heavy in the air, a silent promise of a future burdened by guilt and a forbidden desire.

Chapter 9

Deeper in Desire's Tangled Web

The memory of his passionate encounter with Kajal haunted Usman, leaving him trapped in a whirlwind of conflicting emotions. Guilt gnawed at him, a constant reminder of his betrayal of his brother, Farhan.

Yet, the thrill of the forbidden fruit also lingered, a sweet poison that coursed through his veins.

As Usman ruminated on his recent transgression, his inner angel emerged, his voice filled with sorrow and condemnation. "How could you sink so low?" he chided. "You sinned with your brother's wife. Have you no shame?"

But Usman's devil was quick to counter, his words laced with a seductive allure. "That was the most incredible feeling of your life," he whispered.

"You gave Kajal what she truly wanted. She's been longing for you for a long time."

Usman's mind raced, torn between the two opposing voices. He shrugged his head, unable to reconcile the conflicting emotions.

Switching off the television, he retreated to his bedroom, leaving the turmoil behind. Meanwhile, in Farhan and Kajal's bedroom, a different kind of tension simmered. Kajal rebuffed Farhan's advances, her mood sullen and distant.

Farhan, growing increasingly frustrated, questioned her behavior. "Is there something wrong?" he asked, his voice laced with concern.

Kajal, her voice devoid of emotion, replies "It's just my period."

Farhan, sensing her disinterest, turned off the light, his heart heavy with disappointment.

Usman, burdened by the guilt of his illicit affair, sought solace in the company of his friends. To escape the torment, he turned to the addictive world of pornography, his growing libido fueling his descent into depravity.

Days turned into weeks, and the weight of his actions continued to bear down on Usman. One afternoon, Shahida received a call from her mother, Tabassum, who in her frail voice expressed her longing to see her grandchildren.

Shahida, sensing her mother's declining health, agreed to send her children to visit.

Farhan, Kajal, and Usman arrived at their grandmother's villa on a Tuesday morning. While Farhan rushed to work, Kajal and Usman spent quality time with their grandmother, catching up on some wholesome family banter over tea and homemade cookies.

After a hearty lunch, Kajal insisted on clearing the table and washing the dishes. Usman's grandmother, exhausted, retired to her room for a nap.

As Usman lay on the bed in the guest room, Kajal entered, her face etched with tension.

"Usman, we need to stop," she pleaded. "This is wrong. We must fear Allah and be faithful to Farhan."

But Usman, his desire overwhelming his conscience, stood up and forcefully pushed Kajal onto the bed. Kajal, stunned and terrified, was momentarily paralyzed.

"You're a liar," Usman growled, his voice low and menacing. "You want me. You don't love Farhan. Stop pretending to repent."

Kajal struggled to break free from his grip, her protests falling on deaf ears.

Usman, consumed by passion, was unrelenting as he pulled her towards him, his free hand roaming over her neck, shoulders, before grabbing at her breasts.

At the same time, he sucked her into a passionate lip-lock. An aroused Kajal made one last feeble attempt to escape her brother-in-law's violation of her modesty but to her surprise, she was beginning to like what was happening to her body, and seconds later, she was digging her nails into his shoulders and back. They were both on the bed now.

The encounter got much too hot for an excited, albeit uninitiated Usman, and he reached an orgasm before ejaculating in his underpants.

A completely out-of-breath Kajal drew away from Usman and ran into her room.

Usman walked clumsily to the washroom to clean himself up and change into laundered underwear.

He then spent the entire evening chain-smoking before going to a cybercafe to watch porn.

Returning home, he was asked by his anxious grandmother about his absence to which he replied that he had gone to visit an old school acquaintance a couple of streets away.

After dinner, the married couple retired to their bedroom, while Tabassum and Usman went to their respective rooms.

At around half past midnight, Usman, who had been fantasizing about having sex with Kajal and had already masturbated twice, proceeded to the bedroom occupied by the couple.

He carefully pushed the door open. In the light of the starry night, he saw the couple fast asleep with their backs to each other.

As he tiptoed up to Kajal's side of the bed, his heart pounded in his chest even as a thrill of excitement ran through him.

Keeping an eye on his fast asleep brother, he touched Kajal on her cheek. As he saw her eyes open in the darkness, he gestured with his index finger on his lips, pleading with her to keep quiet and be still.

Lowering his head to her face, Usman then kissed her eyes, her lips.

A terrified Kajal, with one eye fixed on her husband, felt a now-familiar excitement run through her body. Suddenly Farhan moved a little bit, causing Usman to flee from the room.

Chapter 10

A Family's Shattered Peace

The rhythmic thud of cricket balls against willow echoed through the neighborhood, a familiar Saturday symphony in Pakistan. Farhan and Usman, brothers bound by blood and the shared love of the game, joined the throng of local boys, their eyes fixed on the cricket pitch.

As the game progressed, Usman noticed a shift in his brother's demeanor. Farhan's usually sharp focus seemed clouded, his movements sluggish. A missed catch, then another, drew Usman's concern.

"You're off your game, bro," Usman remarked during the drinks break, his voice laced with worry. "You've dropped two easy catches. We might lose this match because of it."

Farhan's reply was a somber nod. "I'm just not myself lately," he admitted, his voice barely a whisper.

Usman, sensing a deeper issue, pressed on. "Is everything alright between you and Kajal?" he asked, his tone gentle.

A long, heavy silence followed. Then, Farhan's voice, laden with emotion, broke the stillness. "We've been fighting a lot. I don't know what's happening to her."

Usman, a mixture of empathy and concern, responded, "Bro, if you're going through something, talk to me. Don't bottle it up. Your friends will only make fun of you behind your back, and I won't stand for that."

Farhan's emotional dam broke. Tears streamed down his face as he poured out his heart to his brother. Usman, though troubled by his brother's pain, was also consumed by his own guilt. His secret affair with Kajal, Farhan's wife, was a constant weight on his conscience.

After the match, a distraught Usman sought solace in his mother's arms. "Mom, I need to talk to you," he pleaded, his voice trembling.

"What's wrong, son? Why are you crying?" Shahida asked, her maternal instincts kicking in.

"I want to get married," Usman blurted out, his words surprising his mother.

"Married? What are you talking about? You're still in college!" Shahida exclaimed, her voice sharp. "First, finish your studies. Then, find a good job. Only then can you think about marriage."

Usman, persistent, pleaded with his mother to start looking for a suitable bride. Shahida, though perplexed, agreed to discuss the matter further the next day.

The following morning, as Shahida and Kajal prepared breakfast, the conversation turned to Usman's sudden desire to marry. Shahida, unaware of the turmoil brewing beneath the surface, casually mentioned it to Kajal.

"Usman seems eager to settle down. We should start looking for a suitable girl for him," Shahida suggested.

Kajal, her face a mask of composure, forced a smile. "Sure, Mom. I'll talk to my family."

After lunch, Kajal goes to Shahida's room to check whether she is sleeping or awake. She sees her mother-in-law is indeed fast asleep.

She then enters the living room where Usman is watching a television serial.

Confronting her brother-in-law in an angry tone, Kajal says to Usman, "I heard you want to get married now. What the fuck were you doing with me all along then?

Asking her to calm down, he says: "Enough is enough, I want to stop. My life's fucked up and before long, yours will be as well if we don't stop our madness."

Taking in a deep breath in an effort to camouflage his emotions, he adds: "It's totally wrong, you know, what we've been doing. Whenever I look into Farhan's eyes or talk to him, the thought of what I am doing to his life nearly chokes me to death. Recently, there have been times when I've wanted to kill myself. I feel so guilty."

Interrupting him, Kajal, in an accusing tone, barks out: "It was you who started this, only after which I fell for you. And now you're dumping me. You men are nothing but bastards. After having all the fun you want, you start feeling guilty. Now you're behaving like a Muslim cleric. But you are a devil to the core and I pray to God that you will never be happy."

"I'm sorry," says Usman, adding: "Please try to keep Far-han happy. It's not too late."

It's Kajal's turn to snap back at Usman: "Fuck off. Get the hell out of my sight."

"Better still, I shall move away from your brother's life once and for all. and from your family," she adds before stomping out of the room.

Chapter 11

House Divided

Usman tossed and turned, his mind a whirlwind of thoughts. The recent encounter with his sister-in-law, Kajal, had left him unsettled. It was well past midnight, but sleep was elusive. In a desperate attempt to escape the suffocating atmosphere of his home, he dialed his older brother, Shani, who resided in the UAE.

"Hey bro, how's everything over there?" Usman inquired, his voice laced with a hint of desperation.

Shani, ever the calm and composed brother, assured Usman that all was well on his end. "Is everything okay with you? You sound a bit off," he asked, his concern evident.

Usman hesitated, then blurted out, "I've been thinking about moving to the UAE. Can you help me with a visit visa?"

Shani, surprised by his brother's sudden decision, questioned, "Don't you want to finish your graduation first?"

"No, I need to get out of here. I can't take it anymore," Usman replied, his voice filled with frustration. "Farhan and Kajal are constantly fighting. It's driving me crazy."

Shani, sensing the depth of Usman's distress, gently probed, "What do you mean?"

"They're always at each other's throats. It's a living hell. Please, just help me get that visa," Usman pleaded.

The next morning, the tension in the house was palpable. A heated argument erupted between Farhan and Kajal over a trivial matter – a cold breakfast.

"The breakfast is cold!" Farhan, who had been dressing up for work, exclaimed, his voice sharp. "The least you could do is serve me a hot meal."

Kajal, equally incensed, retorted, "Who asked you to take an hour for dressing up? You should have had your breakfast when it was served. Take it from me, I'm not your bloody servant to heat your breakfast more than once. As it is, I get up early in the morning to prepare it for you and your bloody family."

The argument escalated rapidly, with each insult more cutting than the last.

"What do you mean, you ungrateful woman? I'm the one who slogs the whole day and all I get in return from you is disrespect and back answers. Even a whore has a heart, but not you," Farhan snarled at her, only raising the spat to boiling point.

"I'm surprised you know how a whore ought to be because you're nothing but a frigid and impotent bastard," Kajal, sneeringly, barked back at her husband.

Now enraged, Farhan lunges forward and slaps Kajal across the face. "Get out of my sight!" he roars.

Kajal, her face stinging, vows revenge. "I won't tolerate this abuse any longer. I'm leaving you, you pathetic excuse for a husband."

With tears streaming down her face, Kajal calls her father. "I can't stay here anymore," she blurts out, between sobs. "He hit me."

Her father, alarmed by her distress, assures her that he would come to her aid. "Don't worry, my dear. I'm on my way."

An hour later, Kajal's father arrives at the house. Addressing Usman's parents, he suggests that it would be best for Kajal to stay with him for a while.

Shahida, understanding the gravity of the situation, agrees. "It would be a good opportunity for both of them to reflect on their relationship, especially during Ramadan, which will be upon us soon."

As Kajal packs her belongings, her sense of relief that has washed over her, is somehow diluted by her deep disappointment over Usman developing cold feet in their ongoing affair. Could finally leaving behind the toxic environment that had consumed her life be the best decision?, she ponders.

However, she soon dismisses this thought and with her father by her side, steps out of the house, leaving behind the shattered remnants of her marriage.

Chapter 12

A New Dawn, A New Beginning in the Desert

Usman's family, save for Kajal who was visiting her parents, gathered in the living room, eagerly awaiting the adhan to signal the breaking of the fast (iftar).

Moments after the Maghrib prayer that followed iftar, Usman received a call from his brother Shani, residing in Sharjah, UAE.

"I have wonderful news for you," an overly excited Shani announced. "Your visa for the UAE has been approved, and I've emailed you a scanned copy."

"Wow, so soon?" Usman exclaimed. "When should I book my flight?"

"As soon as possible," Shani replied.

Overjoyed, Usman's parents and his brother Farhan, who had quickly grasped the significance of Shani's call, offered heartfelt thanks and praise to Allah.

As instructed by Shani, Usman promptly booked a flight to Dubai International Airport, where Shani would be receiving him and taking him to his residence in Sharjah.

The day of Usman's departure finally arrived. A large entourage of family and friends gathered at Sialkot airport at around half past midnight to bid him farewell. As the plane took off in the early hours, Usman's heart pounded with a mixture of excitement and trepidation, embarked as he was, on his first-ever flight, domestic or international.

After his momentary tryst with the clouds as seen from the airplane's windows, it took little time for Usman to be captivated by the angelic faces of the cabin crew as they gracefully served beverages and snacks to the passengers. Despite a sleepless night at the airport, his eyes were wide with wonder. A mischievous thought crept into his mind, "Aren't her sexy buttocks atop her shapely body a sight for sore eyes?" his inner voice, the Devil, whispered.

However, his angelic conscience quickly intervened, reminding him, "Have you forgotten the divine grace that has bestowed upon you this opportunity to build a better future? Instead of succumbing to lustful desires, you should be grateful to Allah and remain steadfast in your faith."

"Tauba, tauba, I apologize," Usman muttered, averting his gaze from the cabin crew member.

Upon landing in Dubai, Usman was greeted by his brother Shani, who promptly whisked him away to Sharjah in a taxi. As they journeyed through the city, Usman was awestruck by the towering skyscrapers and the beautifully landscaped roads.

"Bro, Dubai is incredible!" Usman exclaimed. "These buildings are massive. I've heard the world's tallest building is here."

"Yes, I'll show you around the city," Shani replied. "But remember, our primary focus is finding a job. It's quite challenging here."

After a short drive, they arrived at Shani's modest accommodation, a small room in a high-rise building. Usman was surprised to see the room cluttered with clothes strewn across multiple surfaces – walls, bunk beds, flooring, everywhere.

"What's with all these clothes?" Usman inquired.

"Well, rents are exorbitant here, even higher than in many Western countries," Shani explained. "To save money and remit most of our earnings back home, we're forced to share rooms."

"How many people live in this room?" Usman asked.

"Five, sometimes six or seven," Shani replied.

"Wow, despite our meager income back home, we live like kings compared to this," Usman remarked.

"Alright, you'll learn to adapt to both the good, the bad and the ugly in living conditions but for now, rest for a while," Shani said. "I'm heading to work now." He pointed to the kitchen area and said, "Help yourself to the chicken franks, bread, oil, and utensils. I'll be back in the evening."

Left alone, Usman decided to freshen up before a light breakfast. Exhausted from the previous night and the long flight, he quickly drifted off to sleep.

In his dreams, he found himself back at Dubai airport, mesmerized by the alluring sight of fair-skinned, Chinese-featured women (most of whom were from the Philippines, a country that hitherto he'd never heard of. Usman's inner voice, the Devil, was quick to urge him to indulge in the pleasures of this new environment.

However, his angelic conscience intervened once again, reminding him of his family's sacrifices and his promise to support them financially.

He was urged to resist temptation and focus on his goals, primary among them being sponsoring an Umrah pilgrimage to the Holy Land for his beloved parents.

Shani's return from work jolted Usman awake. He had slept for over ten hours, recovering from the exhaustion and lack of sleep over the past 30 hours or so.

It was 11 PM, but the city was still bustling with activity. Shani took Usman to a nearby mall, where Usman was amazed by the sheer size of the stores and the numerous Eid promotions.

Usman couldn't help but notice the women dressed in figure-hugging clothing. His inner voice again tempted him, but his conscience prevailed, urging him to stay focused on his goals and resist temptation.

"Everything alright, Usman?" Shani asked, noticing his brother's contemplative expression.

"Yes, yes, I'm fine," Usman replied, determined to stay on the right path.

Chapter 13

A Step Forward

A week had passed since Usman's arrival in the UAE, and he'd been tirelessly sending out applications. His heart raced as he opened an email inviting him to an interview the next day. Eager to share the news, he called his brother Shani.

"Congrats, bro!" Shani exclaimed, his excitement tempered by a busy workday. "We'll talk later."

Later that evening, Shani listened intently as Usman detailed the interview.

"This is the address," Usman said, pointing at his phone. "I don't know the area. You'd know better."

"It's nearby, but it's safer to take a taxi," Shani advised.

"If it's close, I can walk," Usman insisted, his youthful energy brimming.

Shani provided directions, both for taxi and foot.

The next morning, Usman woke early, took a quick shower, and dressed in his best attire. The room was still dark, and the soft snores of his roommates filled the air as he quietly performed his Fajr prayer. He tiptoed out of the room, not wanting to disturb Shani.

The morning sun beat down as Usman hailed a taxi, but with no luck, he decided to walk. After a grueling 50-minute trek, he finally reached the interview location.

The bustling office lobby was filled with anxious job seekers. Usman found an empty seat next to a strikingly attractive young woman. A mischievous thought crossed his mind.

"Hey, this is your lucky day," his inner voice urged. "Go on, chat her up. She's looking at you."

Usman felt a surge of nervousness as their eyes met. Just then, his name was called. Cursing under his breath, he rushed into the conference room. The interviewer, after a brief glance at his CV, began, "So, Usman, tell us about yourself."

Usman's mind wandered back to the beautiful woman waiting in the lobby but he managed to focus on the interview.

"We'll let you know our decision in a couple of days," the interviewer concluded.

Usman scanned the lobby for the woman but she was gone. Disappointed, he left the building.

Three days later, Usman's hopes were rekindled as he received another interview call. He immediately called his mother.

"Mother, how are you?" he asked.

"Alhamdulillah, I'm good," she replied. "How are you and Shani? Any luck with the job?"

"Actually, I just got a call for another interview," Usman shared. "Please pray for me."

"InshaAllah, you'll find a good job soon. My prayers are with you," his mother assured him.

The second interview went well, and Usman landed the job. As he walked out of the office building, a wide smile spread across his face. He couldn't wait to share the good news with his mother.

"Mother, I got the job!" he exclaimed.

"Alhamdulillah, thank Allah," she replied. "What kind of job is it?"

"It's as an office boy at a printing press in Sharjah," Usman explained.

"Well, my son, I too have good news for you and Shani. Kajal is back home. She returned yesterday."

"I hope they won't fight again," Usman said. "Okay, Mother, I'll talk to you later."

As he ended the call, Usman looked up at the sky. "Thank you, Allah," he whispered. "You've saved me from hell."

Chapter 14

The Weight of Sin

Usman happily balances his duties as an office boy and a worker on the factory floor of a large printing press. He's also excited to move into his brother's room.

After remitting a significant portion of his first salary to his mother, Usman throws a celebratory dinner party for his roommates, keeping only a small amount for himself.

His mother calls to thank him for the remittance. "Your father and I are proud of both you and Shani. May Allah bless you both find good life partners and achieve peace and success."

"Mother, this is the least I can do for my family, by Allah's grace and mercy. Inshallah, I'll save enough money to send you and Dad on Umrah."

As luck would have it, just a day later, a company notice announces the termination of temporary visa holders, including Usman. His heart sinks as he realizes he's lost his job.

Usman calls Shani, "Bro, the company won't renew temporary visas. I've lost my job after only a month and can't afford to return home. Please help."

Shani assures him of a flight ticket back to Pakistan.

Returning home, Usman avoids Kajal. He greets everyone and feigns a back injury to distance himself from her.

That night, Farhan and Kajal have a heated argument, revealing their deep-seated problems. Thankfully, their parents intervene and restore a fragile peace.

The next day, with his parents visiting a sick relative and Farhan away at work, Usman and Kajal are alone at home. Kajal emerges from the bathroom and moves towards Usman, tears in her eyes. She begins to kiss him, but he pushes her away.

"What are you doing? I'm sorry, but it's over. Try to be happy with my brother," says Usman in a firm voice.

"I can't," Kajal replies.

"You have to. He's your husband."

"But I love you. You made me fall in love with you. I miss your touch, your hands on my breasts, your lips on mine. Oh God."

Frustrated, Usman shouts, "Don't talk like that. I struggle to control myself. Please, don't awaken the devil inside me."

Stepping back, he adds, "I regret what I did. Please go. Let's not start this again."

Kajal advances, clinging to him.

"For God's sake, no," Usman pleads.

But lust overpowers him, and they kiss passionately. The kiss intensifies, and Usman's desire reaches its peak.

He bites Kajal's left nipple lightly through her kameez and and lets off a moan. Not having had enough of her paramour, she begs to be laid. That's when Usman reaches a premature orgasm and shuddering from face to toe, he ejaculates in his pyjamas.

A noise at the door startles Kajal, and she quickly adjusts her clothes and leaves the room.

Usman's conscience berates him, "You selfish, shameless person. You seek forgiveness by sending your mother on pilgrimage? You'll go to hell if you don't repent. Leave your brother's wife alone."

His devilish side though whispers, "Dude…" but Usman silences it, swearing, "SHUT THE FUCK UP in an angry whisper!"

His parents return, and Usman takes the groceries from them into the kitchen.

"Mom, Dad, I want to go to Islamabad for an industrial health and safety course. There are many job opportunities in the UAE for people with this qualification. I could apply from there."

Shahida hesitates, "Why not do it here? You just came back. Why leave again?"

"There's no college here offering this course. I can stay with Aunt Farida in Islamabad or live alone in Karachi."

Reluctantly, his parents agree.

Usman moves to Islamabad and in a couple of months, completes the course. To his surprise, he receives an email from a Sharjah-based newspaper offering him a residence visa.

He calls his mother, "Hello, Mother. How's everyone?"

Shahida, with a heavy heart, shares the news of Kajal having filed for divorce.

Usman, secretly relieved, tells his mother about his job offer.

Shahida asks him to visit before leaving for the UAE.

Back home, Usman is warmly greeted by his parents.

"I'm so happy to see you. This house has been so sad lately. Comfort your brother. He's devastated by Kajal's divorce."

Usman finds Farhan lying on the bed. He whispers, "Farhan, you need to be strong. If you can't, how can I face my future? You'll find someone better than Kajal."

Chapter 15

A Seed of Hope

Usman, a young man brimming with aspirations, received his work visa with a mix of anticipation and trepidation. The visa, however, held a surprise. Instead of the promising position he had envisioned, it designated him as a mere loader and unloader at a local newspaper press.

Disappointed but resolute, Usman decided to seize the opportunity. He believed that even the humblest of beginnings could pave the way for greater achievements.

Relocating to Sharjah, Usman shares a room with his brother Shani and another Pakistani national named Ajmal, who also works at the newspaper press.

As Usman diligently fulfills his duties as a loader-unloader, Ajmal notices his meager food intake. Concerned, Ajmal questions Usman about his austere lifestyle.

Usman reveals his heart's desire: to fulfill his mother's dream of performing Umrah within his first year in the UAE. He believed that rigorous self-discipline and repentance were the keys to attaining divine forgiveness. Ajmal, touched by Usman's sincerity, offers words of encouragement and support.

One Friday afternoon, while reading a magazine, Usman stumbles upon an inspiring article about Jim Carrey. The actor's journey from struggling with odd jobs to achieving global fame resonated deeply with Usman. Inspired by Carrey's story, Usman makes a bold decision: he would not remain a mere loader-unloader. He aspires to become a writer, a journalist.

Driven by this newfound ambition, Usman approaches the manager and requests a change in position. Despite the lack of immediate openings, the manager offers him a position as an office boy in the publishing division. Grateful for the opportunity, Usman accepts the offer, eager to climb the career ladder.

Usman's days are filled with a variety of tasks, from cleaning to assisting in the editorial section. He forms a strong bond with a layout designer named Sid, who generously offers to teach him the intricacies of page design. With newfound enthusiasm, Usman immerses himself in learning InDesign and writing short stories and inspirational anecdotes for a weekend column in the company's English newspaper.

As Usman's career journey unfolds, he takes every opportunity to grow and develop his skills. He periodically calls his mother to share his progress, expressing gratitude for her prayers and support. With each passing day, Usman's determination and unwavering belief in himself propels him forward, igniting a spark of hope within him.

Chapter 16

Lust on Skype takes Flight

During his lunch break at work, Usman checked his Facebook page and saw a friend request from a girl named Anum Jawed. The name rang a bell, so he accepted.

Later that night, as Usman was relaxing on his bunk bed, he started a movie on his laptop while chatting with Anum on his phone.

Usman: "Hey, I remember visiting your family in Karachi during the holidays a few years back."

Anum: "You do? You and Farhan were quite the little rascals."

Usman: "And you had a twin sister, right?"

Anum: "You forgot her name, didn't you?"

Usman: "Yeah, tell me."

Anum: "It's Qandeel."

Usman: "Oh, right. How's she doing?"

Usman: "Well, tell me more about yourself. I'm in the UAE now, working."

Anum: "Wow, how's that?"

Usman went to the kitchen to wash dishes and then returned to his room.

Usman: "It's good. Life's okay."

Anum: "Making good money, huh? Why aren't you married yet?"

Usman: "No girl likes me."

Anum: "You're kidding. Any girl would be lucky to have you. You're handsome and have a job in Dubai. Ask me!"

Usman: "Haha, thanks."

Anum: "See you soon, handsome."

Later that night, Usman browsed Anum's Facebook page. He saw many pictures of her and her twin sister, Qandeel. Despite being twins, they looked very different.

While Anum had a plain appearance, Qandeel was stunning, almost model-like.

Usman was immediately drawn to Qandeel's beauty. He wanted to get to know her better and sent her a friend request.

As he clicked the send button, he thought to himself:

"A dog's curved tail, no matter how long it's straightened, will always return to its natural shape. I'm no different. I'm always drawn to physical beauty. Anum was trying to connect with me, but I'm going for the sexier twin sister. Simple. Qandeel is breathtaking."

The next day at work, Qandeel accepted Usman's request. He immediately messaged her.

Usman: "Hi, how are you?"

Qandeel: "I'm fine. Who are you?"

Usman: "You don't know me?"

Qandeel: "No."

Usman thought to himself: "Why did you accept my request then, drama queen?"

Usman: "I'm your cousin, Anwar uncle's son."

Over the following weeks, Usman and Qandeel chatted frequently, discussing their interests, college, work, and her modeling career.

A few weeks later, Usman landed a position as a layout artist for the sports pages of his newspaper.

A month after that, feeling more confident after his promotion, he called his cousin Salman.

Usman: "I think Qandeel is the one, man. She's my lucky charm. Since I met her, I've become a better person and finally got a decent job."

Salman: "Don't be a fool. You've only known her for a few days. How long has it been since you last saw her in person?"

Usman: "I know, but I have a good feeling about her."

That night, as Usman rested in his top bunk, his phone rang. It was Qandeel, calling from her bedroom.

"Are you awake?" she asked, her face filling the screen.

"Just now," he replied. "Is everything okay?"

"I just got home from the hospital," she said. "It's about your aunt. She had some stomach trouble, but she's fine now. We were all scared."

"Oh, I'm relieved to hear that," Usman said. "I wish I could have been there."

"I know," Qandeel replied. "I wish you were here too."

"I'm always there for you," he assured her.

Impulsively, she said, "Hug me."

"Consider it done," Usman replied. "A long, warm hug."

Then, he asked, "Can I kiss you?"

"Kiss me hard," she replied, her voice growing husky.

"Beautiful woman," he said, "I'm kissing you now."

"And then?" she asked, breathlessly.

"I'm cupping your neck with one hand and rubbing your breasts with the other," he described. "It feels incredible."

"And then?" she urged.

"I'm taking off your top," he said.

Her breathing quickened. "What next? I can't wait."

"I've taken off my clothes too," he said.

"Put it in, now," she demanded.

With a grunt, he replied, "I'm deep inside you. Oh God, it feels amazing. So warm, so wet."

Qandeel moaned, "Go on, harder please, Usman. In a moment later, she scream with a shudder from head to toe, "I'm coming.

With a muffled "Aaaghhhhh," Usman reaches a never-before-felt orgasm that has him shaking all over.

"I've never felt like this before," Qandeel whispers to Usman, her voice low and seductive, her craving for raw, online intimacy finally satisfied.

Still shaking from himself reaching a crescendo, Usman blurts out: "Neither have I," only that his voice is now drowned out by his roommate on the lower bunk, who is letting forth a fusillade of abuses in Urdu.

"What the fuck was that? You're shaking the whole room in the dead of night. Can't you let us sleep in peace, you asshole?" his roommate snarled.

"Imran, I could not bear the extreme cooling in the room," Usman lies, in an apologetic tone.

"Fuck you. Get yourself another blanket but don't you dare mess with the air-conditioning," the roommate barked.

Wondering what happened, Qandeel says to Usman: "Go to sleep now, sweet dreams."

"Good night, baby," he replied.

The next morning, Usman made a decision: he wanted to marry Qandeel. But how would he tell his mother? He decided to ask Shani to broach the subject.

"I need to tell you something important," he said to Shani.

"I can tell," Shani replied. "What is it?"

"I like this girl, and I want to marry her," Usman said. "I need you to talk to Mom."

"Who is she? Does she feel the same way about you?" Shani asked.

"Yes, she does," Usman replied. "And you know her."

"Who is it?" Shani asked, intrigued.

"Qandeel," Usman replied.

"Qandeel? Which Qandeel?" Shani asked, confused.

"Uncle Jawed's daughter. The second one. I love her," Usman explained.

"How long have you known her?" Shani asked.

"Not long, but it feels like forever," Usman replied.

Later that day, Shani told Usman, "I talked to Mom, and she's happy. She says the next step is to talk to Qandeel's parents."

Excited, Usman called Qandeel. "I have good news," he said.

"What is it?" she asked.

"Guess," he replied.

"I can't," she said. "Tell me."

"I talked to my brother, and he asked Mom to talk to your parents about our marriage," he said.

"That's good," she replied. "But if my parents say no, I'll have to respect their decision."

"Why would they say no?" Usman asked. "You should hint to them that you love me."

"No, I can't," she said.

"Why not? Don't you love me?" Usman asked, hurt.

Qandeel didn't respond, and Usman, feeling rejected, blocked her.

The next day, he unblocked her, only to notice a text message from her that read: "Usman, I'm sure my parents will say no. They won't want me to move so far away."

Angrily, Usman replied, "I should have known better, you slut."

Qandeel sent him a crying emoji and blocked him. Usman, too proud to reach out, never contacted her again.

Two months later, Usman received a message from his cousin Salman: "Did you hear that Qandeel is engaged?"

Usman sat quietly, realizing with a mix of pain and clarity, "What I thought was love was really just lust."

He wondered how long he could keep chasing the same shallow connections. Deep down, he longed for something real, something lasting. He knew he needed to understand his own heart better, but he couldn't help asking, would he ever find the love he truly sought?

Chapter 17

A Forced Hand

26-year-old Usman is on his first vacation in 2 years. As he steps out of the Sialkot International Airport concourse, the familiar warmth of his homeland envelops him. A tight embrace from his aging parents, Shahida and Anwar, seals his homecoming.

The familiar landscape had transformed. The once sleepy village now boasts freshly paved roads and modern structures. "It's hard to believe two years have passed," Usman remarked, his gaze drawn to the cityscape.

Shahida, however, had a different perspective. "Yes, son, but progress comes at a cost. The air is polluted, and I often find myself unwell." Her voice trailed off as a fit of coughing seized her.

As the evening approached, Shahida's health deteriorated further. A hasty trip to the hospital and a course of treatment later, she was discharged, much to the family's relief.

A few weeks prior to Usman's return, a relative had shared a photograph of a young woman named Faiza with Shahida, suggesting a potential match for her son.

Now, with her health a pressing concern, Shahida was determined to secure Usman's alliance with Faiza.

"Please, son, just look at her picture. For my sake," she pleaded. "The families have already agreed. I don't know how long I have left. Who will care for you when I'm gone?"

Usman, however, was resolute. "Mother, I've told you, I'm not ready for marriage. You say you're not forcing me but indeed you're manipulating me, using your health as leverage."

Curiosity, however, got the better of him. He glanced at the photograph, his eyes drawn to the girl's fair complexion and European-like features. A battle ensued within him.

His Inner voice, the voice of reason, cautioned him, "Don't toy with someone's life." But a darker voice, the voice of temptation, whispered, "White skin, man. Go for it. No harm in checking out a welcoming white pussy."

Reluctantly, Usman agreed to meet Faiza. On the appointed day, Faiza's family arrived, their presence a stark reminder of the impending engagement.

"Mother, what is this? I said I wanted to meet her first," Usman protested.

Shahida, unmoved, retorted, "This is Pakistan, not Dubai. Traditions matter here. And frankly, can't you trust your mother's judgment?"

As the two families engaged in polite conversation, the engagement date was finalized: the 25th of December, Usman's birthday.

Later that evening, as Shahida busied herself with the dishes, Usman voiced his discontent. "Everything is happening so fast, Mother. I wanted to know Faiza better."

Shahida sighed. "You still think you're in Dubai. Times are changing here too."

The day of the engagement has arrived, but Usman is nowhere to be found. He had slipped away to play cricket with his friends.

Anwar, furious, summons his son. "Today is your engagement, and you're playing cricket? Get home now!"

Usman returned, his face devoid of any joy. As the engagement ceremony unfolded, a strange sense of amusement overtook him. As he stood beside Faiza, he remembered his inner devil's words and couldn't help but chuckle.

A cynical smile crept across his face. He had been a pawn in a game orchestrated by societal norms and familial expectations.

Yet, as he witnessed the joy and celebration surrounding him, a glimmer of hope emerged. Perhaps, he thought, this new chapter could mark a fresh beginning, a chance to atone for past mistakes.

Chapter 18

Allure of Forbidden Fruit

A month had passed since Usman's return from vacation. He had settled comfortably into his new role as a layout artist at the Sharjah newspaper. Delighted with his latest creation, a special events page, he asked his friend Sid to film him designing it. The video, a testament to his growing expertise, was promptly shared with his fiancée, Faiza. Thrilled by his accomplishment, she showered him with digital affection, a simple thumbs-up emoji followed by a heart.

Later that evening, as Usman emerged from a local restaurant, he spotted Sid entering a nearby pharmacy with a striking young woman. Her European features and ethereal beauty captivated his gaze. The next day, curiosity piqued, Usman confronted Sid.

"Bro, I saw you last night," Usman began.

"Where?" Sid replied, feigning indifference.

"Outside that pharmacy near the Afghani Kebab Restaurant. I'd just finished dinner but didn't want to disturb you."

"Oh, that was Anya. She's my girlfriend. We were on a date," Sid explained nonchalantly.

"Wow," Usman mused, a tinge of envy in his voice. "I've always dreamed of falling in love and getting married. But now, here I am, already engaged. Where is she from? She's stunning."

"She's Russian," Sid replied. "Met her on social media."

A silent battle erupted within Usman. His inner devil, a cunning whisperer, urged him to seize the moment. "You're not married yet, man. Faiza's far away. Why not enjoy life a little, just like Sid?"

His conscience, however, offered a stern rebuke. "You've made promises to Allah. Don't break them again."

The devil's voice persisted, more persuasive than ever. "You've got months before the wedding. Live a little. The experience will even help you keep Faiza happy.. ..in bed."

Driven by this newfound audacity, Usman began sending friend requests to attractive, single women on Facebook. While most ignored him, a few accepted.

Meanwhile, Usman's conversations with Faiza grew more intimate. Her love for him deepened with each passing day.

"I miss you, Usman, and am waiting for our wedding day. Then you will be mine. I pray to Allah to protect you at all times. How was your day? Missing me?"

Usman: "Al Hamdulillah. Yes I too miss you and even I'm waiting for our wedding to happen. Till then, life in this desert is killing, especially without someone to love you and take care of you."

Faiza: "I will do all the loving and caring when I am with you, Inshallah."

A week Into his digital pursuit, Usman connected with a woman named Sophia. Her profile pictures, showcasing a youthful beauty, intrigued him. She proudly flaunted that she was a mother of two.

Usman thinks to himself, "This babe doesn't look like a mother of two. I think she would be fun to talk to. After all, my marriage to Faiza is months away."

He messages her: "Hi, how are you?"

"I'm fine, and you?" Sophia replies.

"I'm good. Where are you from?"

"Russia," she answers.

"Where do you live now, Dubai or Russia?"

"I used to live in Dubai, but I moved back home."

As their conversation flowed, Usman couldn't shake the feeling that he was on the brink of something dangerous. Yet, the allure of forbidden fruit was too strong to resist.

Chapter 19

A Fractured Heart

Usman's heart pounded with a mixture of joy and dread as Faiza's radiant face filled his screen. Her infectious laughter, a melody to his ears, masked the growing dissonance within him.

"Oh, Usman, I'm simply over the moon!" she gushed. "Your mother is such a darling. She welcomed us with open arms, and her cooking—divine!"

Usman managed a weak smile, his thoughts already wandering to Sophia's virtual embrace. "I know, right? She's quite the chef."

Faiza's eyes sparkled with love and anticipation. "I can't wait to be a part of your family, Usman. Your parents are so warm and loving. Alhamdulillah."

Usman forced a reassuring tone, "I'm glad you feel that way, Faiza. It means the world to me."

Faiza's voice grew tender. "I yearn for your touch, Usman. A love so pure, so profound, I've only dreamed of. Please, let's not wait any longer."

A pang of guilt shot through Usman as he feigned a sympathetic response. "Everything will happen in due time, my love. Just take care of yourself."

Faiza, blissfully unaware of his duplicity, beamed. "I promise to be the healthiest, happiest bride. I love you, Usman. You know that, don't you?"

Usman's heart raced as he stammered a reply, his mind racing with Sophia's image. "Of course, Faiza. I can't wait to be your husband."

With a hasty excuse about kitchen duties, he ended the call, a wave of relief washing over him.

He longed to escape to Sophia's digital world, where he could be someone else, someone free from the chains of commitment.

But fate had other plans. Thirty minutes later, his mother's voice interrupted his reverie. "Usman, Faiza and her parents were delightful. Such a lovely girl, so simple yet so wise. She'll make a wonderful wife. I'm so happy for you, son."

Usman feigned enthusiasm, his mind a whirlwind of conflicting emotions. "That's great, Ma. I'm just a bit hungry, that's all."

His mother's voice softened. "Just remember, son, the sooner you tie the knot, the better. Faiza will take care of you, make sure you're well-fed and loved."

Usman rubbed his temples, a silent plea for patience. "I know, Ma. We'll figure it out soon enough."

With a heavy sigh, he closed his laptop, the weight of his deception pressing down on his shoulders.

As he drifted off to sleep, the haunting echoes of two women's love filled his dreams, a stark reminder of the fractured heart that lay beneath his façade.

Chapter 20

A Virtual Deception

The time had come to transcend the boundaries of the screen. With a trembling hand, he dialed Sophia's number.

"Hi Sophia," he began, his voice barely a whisper.

"Yes, Usman, how are you doing?" she replied, her tone casual.

"Sophia, I've been thinking about you a lot lately, and I've realized something profound. I think I'm in love with you."

A moment of silence hung heavy in the air. "Do you know what you're saying? We've only been video chatting for a few months, and we haven't even met in person," Sophia responded, her voice laced with caution.

"I know," Usman replied, his determination unwavering. "But I trust my heart. I know how I feel about you."

Sophia's hesitation was palpable. "I'm sorry, Usman, but I don't trust men. My past experiences have made me wary. I can't risk getting hurt again."

Usman persisted, his voice filled with sincerity. "Not all men are the same, Sophia. I promise I'll never hurt you."

A flicker of hope ignited in Sophia's eyes. "You seem different, but I'm still cautious. I can't afford to be disappointed again."

Usman's heart ached as he witnessed her pain. "I understand, Sophia. I'll never forget your past. I promise to treat you with the respect and love you deserve."

Sophia's voice softened as she shared her painful memories. "My ex-husband abandoned his responsibilities and neglected our family. I couldn't take it anymore."

Usman offered words of comfort, his voice gentle. "I'm so sorry to hear that, Sophia. Please believe me when I say I'm different. You and your darling daughters would mean the world to me."

Sophia's eyes welled up with tears. "You seem different, but deep down, I fear you'll eventually leave me too."

Usman's resolve strengthened. "I swear on my heart, I won't."

"Only time will tell," Sophia replied, her voice heavy with doubt. "For now, I need to put my children to sleep. Goodnight, Usman."

As the days turned into nights, their virtual intimacy deepened. One evening, Usman, emboldened by his growing affection, crossed a line. "What are you wearing, Sophia?" he asked, his voice laced with desire.

Sophia hesitated. "I'm about to sleep. I usually wear just a shirt and underpants. Why do you ask?"

"Darling, I'd love to see you in those underpants," Usman replied, his voice growing more insistent.

Sophia's initial reluctance gave way to a dangerous curiosity. "The kids are still awake. Maybe later?"

Usman pressed his advantage. "Please, Sophia. I'm begging you."

Reluctantly, Sophia agreed. After her children were asleep, she slipped into the bathroom, removed her shirt, and snapped a few photos. With trembling fingers, she sent the intimate images to Usman.

As Usman's eyes devoured the explicit images, a surge of desire coursed through his veins. He traced the contours of Sophia's body with his fingertips, his heart pounding with anticipation.

The next day, Usman received a call from his mother, Shahida. "Son, we're planning Farhan's second wedding. We'd love for you to take a vacation and get married on the same day."

Usman was taken aback, his mind racing. He blurted out: "I can't take a vacation right now, mother. Work is too busy. Moreover, a couple of my colleagues are already on vacation and so, we are short-staffed but hearty congratulations to Farhan. I'll call him a little later."

Later that very same day, Usman approaches his manager and requests a ten-day leave of absence.

When asked the reason for going on leave, Usman lies that it's because his mother's health is failing. The manager, unaware of the true reason, approves his request.

That night, Usman video-calls Sophia. "I'm taking a vacation next month. I want to come to Russia and see you and your girls. I've saved up enough money for the trip."

Sophia's reaction was muted. Sensing her hesitation, Usman pressed her. "What do you want me to do, love?"

Sophia, her voice tentative, proposed a different plan. "I want to come to Dubai to see you."

Usman's heart soared. "That would be amazing! I'd love to have you here."

"But I don't have the money for the visa or the ticket," Sophia confessed.

Usman, eager to seal the deal, offered to cover all the expenses. "Don't worry, I'll arrange everything. Would you like to bring the kids?"

Sophia declined the offer. "I'll come alone. My mother can take care of the girls."

As the call ended, Usman was filled with a mix of excitement and apprehension. Little did he care to see that he was on the brink of a dangerous affair, a secret love that could shatter his life.

Chapter 21

Tempest of Passion

The night before Sophia's arrival, Usman tossed and turned, his mind a whirlwind of anticipation. His body tingled with a nervous excitement that kept him awake.

Early the next morning, he hurried to the ATM, withdrawing a substantial sum. A dazzling bouquet, a token of his affection, was the next stop. Finally, he met up with his friend Sid, and together they cabbed it to the airport. Usman's heart kept pounding with expectation along the way.

As Usman stepped into the arrivals hall, his gaze swept the crowd, searching for a glimpse of the woman who had captured his heart. When he saw her, a surge of adrenaline coursed through him. Sophia, his dream incarnate, exuded an ethereal beauty that left him breathless. Her smile, a radiant beacon, ignited a fire within him.

"You look stunning," he stammered, handing her the bouquet. "Even more beautiful than in the pictures."

"Thank you," she replied, her voice a soft melody. "You look good too."

As they drove to the hotel, conversation flowed effortlessly, as if they had known each other for years. Sid bid them farewell, leaving the lovebirds to their own devices.

Inside the room, a palpable tension filled the air. "How's the room?" Usman asked, breaking the silence.

"It's lovely, cozy," Sophia replied, her eyes sparkling with mischief.

"You should rest," he suggested, though his mind was far from rest.

When he returned from the bathroom, Sophia was lying on the bed, her eyes inviting. As he approached, she whispered, "Do you want to kiss me?"

The kiss ignited a passion that consumed them both. Soon, their clothes were discarded, and they surrendered to the primal urge. The room was filled with soft moans and gasps as they explored each other's bodies.

"This is heaven," Usman murmured, lost in the moment. "You're so beautiful, so perfect."

But their passion was cut short by a sudden realization. Sophia's face clouded with concern. "You didn't use protection?" she asked, her voice sharp.

Usman, overwhelmed by the intensity of the moment, had forgotten. "I'm so sorry," he apologized, his heart heavy with guilt.

Despite the mishap, their connection remained strong. They spent the rest of the day exploring Dubai, their love growing deeper with each passing moment.

As they walked along the pristine beaches of Jumeirah, Usman couldn't help but feel like he was living a dream.

Later that night, as they lay in bed, Sophia revealed a painful secret. As she struggled with depression, a consequence of a failed marriage and the challenges of single motherhood, she had become dependent on prescription drugs. But with Usman by her side, she confessed to him that she felt a glimmer of hope.

Touched by her vulnerability, Usman vowed to be her strength, her protector. He promised to love and cherish her and her daughters through thick and thin. And as they drifted off to sleep, hand in hand, Usman revelled in the warm feeling that their love story had only just begun.

Next morning, the sun's golden rays kissed Usman's eyelids, a gentle nudge to awaken him from his dream. Sophia's hand, warm and inviting, traced patterns on his chest. Her voice, a soft whisper, broke the morning silence, "Good morning, my love."

A surge of desire swept through him. "Oh, God," he murmured, a shiver running down his spine, "this feels incredible. It's a dream I never wanted to end."

Their bodies intertwined once more, their passion a tempestuous dance. The world outside faded away, replaced by a universe of sensation and ecstasy.

Afterwards, Usman prepared breakfast, his movements imbued with a newfound tenderness. Sophia captured the moment, her camera clicking away. "Why the pictures?" he asked, a hint of amusement in his voice.

"I want to show my mother how well you're taking care of me," she replied, a mischievous glint in her eye.

As they ate, their fingers interlaced. A gentle kiss, a stolen glance, spoke volumes of their love. "I read somewhere that many women don't enjoy oral sex," Usman ventured, his voice hesitant.

Sophia smiled. "It depends on the woman and the man. But when love is involved, anything is possible."

"Do you love me?" he asked, his heart pounding in his chest.

"Yes, that's why I'm here," she replied, her gaze unwavering.

"You've never actually said those words before," he mused.

"Oh, haven't I?" she teased. "Remember yesterday, when you were... well, you know?"

A blush crept across his face. "Oh, right. You did say it. How could I forget? Please, say it again. It means the world to me."

"I love you, I love you, I love you," she repeated, her voice filled with affection. "Is that enough, you silly boy?"

"Where should we go today?" he asked, his eyes sparkling with anticipation.

"I'm tired," she replied, "let's stay in bed. We can go out tomorrow."

As she changed into a shirt and jeans, Usman began cleaning up the dishes. His phone rang, his mother's voice seemed to fill the room.

"Usman, how are you? I haven't heard from you in two days. Where have you been? Are you okay?"

"I'm fine, Mother. How's everyone at home?"

"Alhamdulillah, everyone's good. By the way, Uncle Sajid and Aunt are planning to go on Hajj next month."

A pang of guilt shot through Usman. He had spent a significant amount of money on Sophia, money that could have been used to send his parents on Hajj. "I see," he replied, his voice heavy with regret. "I wish I could send you too, but I need to save more money. It's my dream to send you and Dad on Hajj one day."

"We have Farhan's wedding coming up. It would have been nice if you two married at the same time," his mother said, her disappointment evident.

"Not again, Mother. I've told you, I need to save more money first."

"Alright, son. Take care. Goodbye."

A silent battle raged within Usman. His inner angel chided him, "You hypocrite. You claim to love your mother, yet you've been so selfish. You've spent more on Sophia than you would have on your mother's Hajj. And how do you treat Faiza? You don't even answer her calls. You're turning into a monster."

His inner devil countered, "Silence him.

You have a life too. If you hadn't acted quickly, Sophia wouldn't be here. Faiza was never right for you. Sooner or later, you'll have to tell them the truth."

Sophia, sensing his turmoil, asked, "What's wrong, Usman?"

"Nothing," he replied, forcing a smile. "Let's go."

They spent the day shopping, indulging in retail therapy. Usman carried the bags, his strength a testament to his love.

"You're the first man to treat me like a queen," Sophia said, her voice filled with gratitude.

"You mean everything to me," he replied, his heart overflowing with affection.

A video call from Sophia's mother interrupted the moment. They exchanged greetings, and Sophia introduced Usman to her children.

"Do you want to come stay with me?" Usman asked the children, his voice filled with warmth.

"If Mama comes too," they replied in unison.

Sophia ended the call, turning to Usman. "Thank you for being so kind to my daughters and mother. They seem to like you."

"I love them like my own," he replied, his voice sincere.

As they lay in bed, Sophia broke the silence. "Usman, I'm leaving in three days. Would you like me to come back?"

"Of course," he replied, his voice filled with longing. "I can't bear to be without you."

"I've been thinking," she said, "maybe you could save some money and send me a three-month visit visa. I could work and then apply for a residence permit. After that, it would be easier to bring the kids."

"That's a great plan," he exclaimed. "Let's do it. But first, let's make love one last time."

Their passion consumed them, a fiery dance of love and desire. The days that followed were a whirlwind of intimacy and indulgence. Usman showered Sophia with gifts, his love for her boundless.

As the day of her departure drew near, a heavy weight settled on his heart. "These have been the best days of my life," Sophia said, her voice filled with emotion. "Thank you for everything. Take care of yourself."

He watched her pack, his heart aching with longing. He knew that life without her would be a barren wasteland.

Chapter 22

A Fractured Commitment

Usman, heart pounding with a mix of excitement and dread, exited the airport, the echoes of Sophia's laughter still ringing in his ears. He dialed Sid's number.

"You old dog, how's the vacation treating you?" Sid's jovial voice greeted him.

"Just finished, man," Usman replied, his tone turning serious. "I need a favor."

"Shoot," Sid said, ever the loyal friend.

"I blew my savings man. Need some cash when I get back."

Usman had grown weary of the communal living, the lack of privacy a constant irritant. With Sophia, he craved solitude, a space where their love could blossom undisturbed. He moved into a smaller, quieter room, the extra rent a price worth paying for the peace it afforded.

As he settled into his new abode, his mother's voice intruded. "Son, when are you coming home? We need to finalize the wedding date. Faiza's family keeps inquiring."

Usman hesitated, his heart heavy. "Mother, I've changed my mind about marriage. I need time to stabilize financially and find a better job."

"But Usman, marriage will alleviate your burdens. Faiza will be your support."

"Let me think. Besides, work commitments prevent me from taking a vacation."

"Don't make excuses. Apply for leave and come next month."

"Mother, I'm serious. If they can't wait, they should find someone else. I've made my decision."

"Are you out of your mind? Faiza's father is ill, and she's distraught. Have you any sense?"

"Give me a few days to think. Please, Mother. Let me work."

"I expect a different answer next time."

Later, on a video call with Sophia, Usman poured out his heart. "My parents are forcing me into a marriage I don't want. Only you, my love, matter. Let's marry in Russia, away from their interference."

Sophia's eyes, filled with love and concern, softened his resolve.

"My love, I wish I had the means. You'll have to handle the finances."

"Don't worry, darling. I'll take care of everything. Our wedding will be perfect."

Another call from his mother interrupted his daydream. Faiza's father's condition had worsened, and she was unwell. She'd even complained to her parents about his indifference.

"Answer her calls, Usman. Show some respect for your future wife," his mother demanded.

Far from complying with his mother's diktat, a frustrated Usman blocked Faiza's calls and social media accounts.

The next day, his uncle called, his voice stern. "Usman, be honest. Do you still want to marry Faiza?"

Hesitantly, Usman confessed his love for Sophia. He sent his uncle pictures of them together, a stark declaration of his intentions.

"You've betrayed your family. May Allah guide you, but I'm afraid, as far as I see, you're on your way to ruining your life," his uncle said, his voice filled with angst and disappointment.

Usman, resolute in his decision, blocked calls from his parents, siblings, and even his brother Shani. He was ready to embrace his new life, consequences be damned.

Chapter 23

The Price of Betrayal

Kamran, a man burdened with a heavy secret, trudged towards his nephew's house. The weight of the news he carried was palpable, a dark cloud looming over the family. Shahida, Usman's mother, greeted him with a concerned look, her intuition sensing the storm brewing.

"Usman has fallen deeply for another woman," Kamran confessed, his voice heavy with sorrow. "He's ended his engagement with Faiza."

The news sent shockwaves through the family. Anwar, Usman's father, was stunned. Farhan, his brother, was furious. Shahida, heartbroken, could only weep.

"We must inform Faiza's family," Kamran declared, his voice resolute.

Kamran broke the devastating news to Faiza's family, their faces contorting with disbelief and anger. Haneef, Faiza's father, was particularly incensed.

"That coward, Usman, has shattered our daughter's life!" he roared, his eyes burning with rage. "He owes us an explanation!"

Kamran, unable to reach Usman, could only offer his sympathy. Haneef, consumed by anger and despair, decided to confront Usman's family directly.

A heated argument erupted between the two families, accusations flying like darts from Haneef's side. Shahida and Anwar, overwhelmed by guilt and shame, could only listen in silence.

Meanwhile, Faiza, alone and heartbroken, received yet another rejection from Usman. He'd blocked her calls. The weight of his betrayal was too much to bear. As she lay on her bed, a wave of despair washed over her. A sudden, sharp pain shot through her body, leaving her paralyzed from the waist down on her left side.

Her parents, returning home from the confrontation, found their daughter motionless, tears streaming down her face. Panic-stricken, they rushed her to the hospital.

The doctor's diagnosis was devastating. Faiza had suffered trauma-induced paralysis. The emotional turmoil caused by Usman's betrayal had taken a physical toll on her body.

Haneef, consumed by anger and grief, tried repeatedly to reach Usman, but his calls went unanswered. In a final attempt to confront him, he called Anwar.

"Your son has destroyed my daughter's life!" Haneef thundered. "He deserves to pay for his sins!"

Anwar, filled with remorse, could only apologize. He promised to find his son and make amends. But as he tried to reach Usman, he too was met with silence.

Chapter 24

A Digital Delusion

The sterile office cabin was Usman's sanctuary, a quiet haven where he could escape the mundane. Today, however, it was a stage for a different kind of performance, a digital drama unfolding on the screen of his laptop. He logged into Skype, his heart pounding with anticipation. But the dot beside Sophia's name was stubbornly offline.

A pang of worry shot through him. He quickly typed a message, his fingers dancing across the keyboard. But the message remained unread, a digital ghost in the ether. A futile attempt to reach her followed, only to be met with the cold, stark reality of an insufficient balance.

The afternoon sun beat down mercilessly as Usman rushed to a nearby store, his mind a whirlwind of thoughts. He returned, phone recharged, and dialed her number.

"Hello darling, how are you? Is everything okay? You were not online and I got worried," Usman's voice, laced with concern, echoed through the line.

"I'm fine, I came over to my brother's house. There's no Internet here. Don't worry, we'll talk when I go back home," Sophia's voice, though polite, carried a distant tone.

"Okay, when will you be back at your place?" Usman persisted.

"Maybe tomorrow, don't call me. Making overseas calls is so expensive. We'll chat later," she said, her voice cutting through the line like a knife.

That night, Usman tried again, this time via video call.

"Where have you been? I've been trying to reach you for hours," he asked, his voice filled with frustration.

"I'm busy. You know I have two kids to take care of, and it takes all of my time," Sophia replied, her tone sharp and dismissive.

"Sorry, darling," Usman apologized, his voice softening.

"Usman, don't just 'darling' me. You should understand," she retorted.

"Okay, but…" he tried to explain, but she cut him off.

"Bye then," she said, ending the call abruptly.

Usman's heart sank. A silent battle raged within him, a conflict between his angelic and demonic inner voices.

"This had to come. By not reciprocating Faiza's sincere love, you were already on the road to messing your life big time," the angelic voice warned.

"What nonsense," the devilish voice scoffed. "Don't read too much into it. It's just her period, dude. No big deal."

The following day, Usman, fueled by a mix of curiosity and desperation, delved into Sophia's Facebook profile.

He discovered a second account, a hidden facet of her digital identity. He reached out, his heart pounding with a mix of hope and fear.

"Do you use another Facebook account?" he asked, his voice barely a whisper.

"Yes, this was my old one, which I had stopped using because I had forgotten the password. But recently, I remembered it, so I started reusing it. Why are you asking?" Sophia replied, her tone evasive.

"Just asking… Sorry," he mumbled, his heart heavy.

At work, Usman shared his concerns with his friend Sid. Sid, a realist, offered a sobering perspective.

"Honestly, let me tell you, bro, I think it's high time you call off this relationship. She seems to have no feelings for you. In fact, I would go ahead and say she doesn't seem to care about you at all," Sid said bluntly.

"No, bro, she loves me. Maybe she's gone into depression. I've seen her taking pills when she was here with me," Usman insisted.

"Look how rudely she talks to you. Any man would be offended by that tone. I can only give you advice, following it or not is up to you," Sid replied.

Usman, torn between love and logic, was on the brink of despair. He sought solace in the gym, pouring his energy into physical exertion. Yet, his mind was consumed by thoughts of Sophia and her mysterious second account.

Also, Sid's advice about moving on haunts him and somewhere at the back of his mind he begins to wonder what is transpiring back home in Pakistan, what with his uncle Kamran having broken the news of his relationship with Sophia to the family.

Out of curiosity, he decides to contact his uncle and find out what's going on. After taking his uncle off the blocked list, he calls him.

Usman to Kamran: "Hello, uncle! How are you and the family doing?"

Kamran: "How dare you call me after having blocked my calls for over a week? Moreover, you have the gall to enquire about family? Do you know what your thoughtless actions have resulted in so far?"

Usman: "Uncle, please tell me."

Kamran: "Faiza has taken very ill, in fact she's lying in a hospital bed, paralysed. That's because she took your rejection of her very badly. Her parents are anguished as much as your parents are shamed by your frivolous ways."

Usman fakes an apology but at the same time he tells his uncle that he was only being led by his heart.

"What's happening with you at present?" Kamran asks his nephew.

Usman lies: "Everything is good, very good. Uncle, I'll keep you posted on my plans with Sophia."

He adds, "Once things settle down, which I hope will happen sooner than later, I'll keep in constant touch with my family. I hope you understand."

Chapter 25

An Illusion Finally Shattered

Usman is left with mixed feelings after his call with his uncle Kamran ended. His inner demon, is quick to whisper over his left shoulder: "Dude, it's Sophia you should be focused on. You know now that your Pakistani fiancée – albeit with a white pussy that's been your life-long craving – is out of your life. Imagine spending your days with a maimed and broken creature."

But a saner voice, his conscience, countered: "Being the prime cause of Faiza's present desperate condition, you should be praying for her well-being. And seeking forgiveness for your ill intentions. You only called your uncle to see if another white woman was still an option. Beware brother, you're getting nowhere with an illusion of love."

Ignoring his conscience, Usman is consumed by a need to know Sophia's secrets. He creates a fake Facebook account in her name and sends friend requests to a handful of her male contacts.

Frustrated and restless, he goes for a run. As he pounds the pavement, he keeps muttering to himself, "No, no, no, Sophia, I trust you. I love you. You're mine forever."

Back in his room, he logs into the fake account. A message from a man named "Awesome Dude" catches his eye.

"Hi sweetheart. Seems like you've got a new ID. Just for me?"

Usman, pretending to be Sophia, replies, "Hi handsome. Well, I've been thinking about you."

A series of sexually charged messages follow, revealing a deep, intimate connection between Sophia and this man. Usman's heart pounds hard as he reads the explicit details.

Rage consumes him. He slams his laptop shut and storms out of his apartment. In the elevator, he repeatedly mutters curses, "You bitch. You only cared about the holiday, the gifts, the money. What an idiot I was to think you loved me."

Later, as he and his friend Sid are waiting at a traffic signal on their way home, Usman, his mind still clouded by thoughts of Sophia, narrowly escapes a speeding car as he begins crossing the road even before the pedestrian signal turns green.

"What the hell you think you're doing?" Sid yelled. "You could have died!"

"I was thinking about Sophia," Usman replies, tears welling up in his eyes.

"Even if you died, nothing would change for her," Sid says bluntly.

"No, no, bro, I know Sophia. Whatever happened with that guy was in the past. She loves me now."

"Does she? Seriously? Dude, I give up on you."

The next day, Usman books a flight to Moscow and emails Sophia. He's over the moon when she calls. However, his heart quickly sinks when Sophia reveals that she cannot host him due to family commitments, before abruptly cutting the call.

Usman, confused and hurt, tries to reach her, but she ignores his many calls. Desperate and alone, he spirals into a deep depression.

Holding his head in his hands, a forlorn Usman cries out: "O God… O God… Why is Sophia doing this to me? Why has she left me like a bag of thrash? I've never felt so fucked up in all my life…. I don't think it's worth living any more…"

Even so, clinging to a flicker of hope, Usman compulsively checks his phone every few minutes, yearning for a message from Sophia. Yet, the screen remains stubbornly silent, offering no solace.

Usman paces his room, from time to time keeps pulling his hair, and crying out loud. The bathroom mirror reflects a broken man, haunted by the ghost of his lost love.

Chapter 26

The Weight of Regret

The weight of the world presses down on Usman. Sleep is a fleeting visitor, denied by the gnawing anxiety of a recent heartbreak. Sophia, the woman who promised forever, has vanished from his life as abruptly as she entered it.

Tonight, sleep begins to claim him when his phone's insistent ring shatters the fragile peace. It is two in the morning. His uncle Kamran's voice, heavy with sorrow, delivers the devastating news. Farhan, his brother, is gone.

"Farhan… gone?" Usman echoes, disbelief and horror warring within him.

Kamran breaks the silence. "Everyone in your household has been frantically trying to reach you for the past hour. You'd blocked them all, thank God you'd unblocked me last week."

"Your father informed me moments ago, and I immediately called you. You must leave for Pakistan at once."

Usman's voice, filled with shock, barely forms a question. "How did it happen?"

Kamran's tone is somber. "He took his own life. Life had become unbearable for him, even with his second marriage. In fact, it seemed he'd turned to drugs towards the end of his troubled marriage to Kajal, and he never fully recovered from that ordeal."

Usman's sobs echo through the phone.

Kamran continues, his voice steady despite the gravity of the news, "His second wife told us he'd been acting erratically, neglecting his work, and wandering the neighborhood aimlessly, often under the influence of dope. Just two days ago, he was found unconscious in a nearby drain."

Usman's weeping intensifies.

Kamran adds, "He was revived, but tragically, early this morning, around 1:15 or 1:30 AM, while his wife slept, he hanged himself from the ceiling fan.

The heat in the room caused the fan to stop, awakening his wife, who discovered him hanging motionless from the fan, albeit a bit too late. He was gone."

Usman's sobs continued, unrelenting.

Kamran urges Usman, "Don't waste any time. Book the first available flight to Pakistan. Your brother Shani is already on his way."

The call ends.

Usman rushes to the airport, securing a 5 AM flight to Sialkot. His mind turns to his mother. He recalls blocking her number and quickly unblocks her and the rest of his family. As soon as he unblocks his mother, her call comes through.

Shahida (sobbing, her cries intensifying): "Usman…"

"Mother, I know about Farhan. Uncle called. I'm at the airport. I'm coming."

His mother's wailing continues. Usman hesitates to end the call, and his father's voice cuts through.

"Where have you been? We've been trying to reach you for over three hours. Your brother Farhan… he's gone. Come home immediately."

Amidst his mother's anguished screams, Usman tells his father, "I told Mother I'm at the airport. I'll be home in about three hours."

"You must hurry if you want to see your brother's face one last time before the burial."

Overwhelmed by grief, Usman books the earliest flight to Pakistan. The plane journey is a blur, his mind racing with a whirlwind of emotions. Guilt, sorrow, and a deep sense of responsibility weigh heavily on his soul.

Upon his arrival, the house is a somber tableau of mourning. His mother, inconsolable, weeps her heart out. His father, a man of stoic silence, wears a mask of grief. The funeral, a solemn affair, is a stark reminder of the fragility of life.

(THE PRESENT DAY – 9pm)

Later that night, as Usman sits alone in his room, his sister, Farida, brings him a cup of tea. A tense silence hangs between them, broken only by the soft ticking of the clock.

"Why wasn't I told about Farhan's problems?" Usman asks, his voice barely a whisper.

Farida hesitates, her eyes filled with compassion. "We didn't want to add to your stress. You are always so busy, so far away."

Usman's gaze hardens. "And what about Faiza? I ruined her life. I destroyed her hopes and dreams."

Farida's expression turns somber. "She is devastated. Her father is hospitalized due to the stress. And now, she lies paralyzed with no hope of a recovery anytime soon, or that's what the specialists say."

A wave of guilt washes over Usman. He has been so self-absorbed, so reckless, that he has shattered the dreams and caused irreparable damage to the lives of those who love him.

As the weight of his sins bears down on him, a dark thought creeps into his mind. Is there any point in continuing? He has failed as a brother, a son, and a man.

With a heavy heart, Usman stands up and walks towards the terrace. Farida, sensing his despair, rushes after him. She hands him a sealed envelope, a final message from Farhan.

As Usman stands on the terrace, the city lights twinkling in the distance, he contemplates the abyss. He keeps walking around the terrace for the next couple of hours, sometimes breaking into a jog, completely immersed in his sorrow.

He shouts out to the overhead moon: "My rotten life has to end once and for all.. ..Fuck everyone.. ..Fuck Shah Rukh Khan and his romance-laced movies.. ..Fuck that bitch Sophia.. ..Fuck myself.. ..I want to fuckin' die.. ..get the fuck out of this fucked-up world."

As a fleeting cloud eclipses the moon, the weight of his past mistakes, the pain of his present, and the uncertainty of his future, threaten to consume him.

Chapter 27

It's The Time of Reckoning

The late evening sky, a canvas painted with hues of twilight, is alive with the cacophony of crows and sparrows. They dart and dive, their silhouettes stark against the fading light. Below, the city pulses with anticipation, a tapestry of twinkling lights illuminating the night. It is Independence Eve, a time for joy and celebration. Yet, in a quiet corner of this bustling metropolis, a different story unfolds.

Usman, his heart heavy with a secret burden, withdraws Farhan's letter from its envelope. His fingers trace the familiar script, a bittersweet reminder of a bond once strong, now shattered. As he begins to read, a wave of emotion washes over him.

"Dearest Usman," Farhan's words, etched on the page, pierces his soul. "A few months ago, Kajal, my ex-wife, confessed to an affair with you. In a moment of rage, I yearned to end your life. Had you been within my reach, I fear I might have succumbed to that dark impulse, despite our bond of brotherhood."

The letter continues, each word a dagger to Usman's heart. "Your betrayal was a wound that festered. I struggled to survive, haunted by your deceit. I know this revelation will devastate you, perhaps even drive you to despair. But that would be the easy way out. You must endure the consequences of your actions."

"For the sake of our parents, I impose this punishment upon you: a life of remorse and the constant struggle for redemption. Honor their memory and mine by seeking Allah's forgiveness."

A torrent of tears streams down Usman's face as he reads the final words. "How deeply I loved you, and how intensely I hated you. But now, as death approaches, I find myself filled with love once more. I love you, brother. I love you so much."

A shiver runs through Usman's body as he folds the letter and slips it back into his pocket. The weight of the past, a crushing burden, threatens to consume him. He rises, his movements slow and deliberate. As he approaches the terrace door, a figure emerges from the darkness. It is Haneef, Faiza's father.

"Uncle Haneef, I wanted to meet you."

"And I wanted to meet you as well, you stinking bastard," Haneef snarls, his voice a venomous hiss. With a swift motion, he draws a pistol from his waistband and points it directly at Usman.

A gunshot echoed through the night, shattering the silence and the hope of a new dawn for Usman.